ZANDER BINGHAM

www.greenrhinomedia.com

First Printing: December 2019

Green Rhino Media LLC
228 Park Ave S #15958
New York, NY 10003-1502
United States of America

www.jackjonesclub.com

ISBN 978-1-949247-16-9 *(Paperback - US)*

ISBN 978-1-949247-18-3 *(Paperback - UK/AU)*
ISBN 978-1-949247-17-6 *(eBook - US)*
ISBN 978-1-949247-19-0 *(eBook - UK/AU)*

Library of Congress Control Number: 2019919485

DEDICATION

This book is dedicated to my youngest son, Greyson, whose love of trains (and the creative names he comes up with for them) inspired me to write this book.

This one's for you, Grey, my boy.

CONTENTS

ACKNOWLEDGMENTS

Diana, you are the wind in my sails – thank-you for continuing on this amazing writing journey with me.

Karen, thank-you for bringing the story to life with your wonderful illustrations.

Claire, never make apologies for being the 'consistency police' – Jack, Emma, Albert and I are grateful for your support, and for pointing out if something doesn't quite make sense.

Greyson, your love of trains and your enthusiasm for learning more about how they work is a never-ending joy to watch.

Xavier, thanks for being my 8-year-old audience; listening to the drafts of this story and sharing your wonderful feedback along the way.

All the Jack Jones readers, thank-you from the bottom of my heart for joining the journey – I'm so glad to be able to create more adventures for these characters and it's been a real thrill having you along for the ride.

CHAPTER ONE

Jack hurried to keep up with his parents, trying not to lose sight of them as they crossed the main hall of Central Station.

His best buddy Albert and younger sister Emma shuffled closely behind him as they wove through the crowds and tried to avoid being swallowed up by the sea of people around them.

"So, what's this all about anyway?" Jack called to his parents over the hustle and bustle as he glanced at the soaring arched ceiling overhead, admiring the grand old building.

Theodore and Penelope Jones stepped into a quiet alcove as the children caught up.

"Like your dad said, it's a surprise. Come on, we're almost there." Mrs. Jones smiled warmly, her brown hair swaying as she turned and winked at Jack through her glasses.

"Well it's pretty obvious we're getting on a train, Mom." Emma looked at her mother with a cheeky grin, her gymnastics classes proving useful as she gracefully dodged other busy travelers. "But which one is it—and where will it take us?"

"That's the exciting part! We need to find platform ten. Keep up, kiddos," Mr. Jones encouraged, as they hurried past a large sign that read *Platform 8*.

"Are we going on one of those super-fast bullet trains?" Albert guessed excitedly, pushing up his thick, black-rimmed glasses.

"Not quite," Mr. Jones replied thoughtfully.

"Hey, there's platform ten... but there's no train." Jack shrugged as he ran a hand through his thick blond hair and pointed toward the empty track.

"I said we needed to *find* platform ten, not that it was our destination. There. That's where we're meeting Professor Coleman." Mr. Jones nodded toward a large black door labeled 'Maintenance Area.'

"Wait a minute, that sign says 'Crew Access Only'. Are you sure we're supposed to be going in there?" Albert asked curiously.

"Professor Coleman? What's going on guys?" Jack pushed up the sleeves of his lucky jacket and stared back and forth between his parents.

3

Mrs. Jones chuckled while her husband stepped to the door and rapped his knuckles against it, knocking loudly as the three confused kids looked on.

"All is about to be revealed," Mrs. Jones replied, her eyes twinkling.

"So, who's this guy, Professor Coleman?" Albert asked in a hushed voice.

"Oh, Professor Coleman's really cool. He's an engineer who teaches at the same university as my parents. They've been friends for like *ever*," answered Jack.

"And he's always up to something awesome..." Emma added thoughtfully.

"Yeah, last time we saw him he took us hot air ballooning." Jack grinned at the memory.

"And remember the vintage race car he restored?" Emma asked.

"Right! That *was* totally cool! Albert, seriously, I got to drive in a 1964 MG. It was awesome! *Vrrrmm!*" Jack laughed as he scrunched his face and steered a pretend wheel with his hands.

"Wow, neat!" Albert replied, "I remember you telling me about it, I can't believe I was away for that. So, I guess no hot air balloons today though...?"

"Your guess is as good as mine. Professor Coleman gets up to all kinds of random things... but since we're at a train station, hot air ballooning is probably *off track*, get it?" Jack grinned.

"Oh, ha ha, Jack!" Emma giggled.

Albert shook his head and smiled. Just then, the maintenance door opened with a groan and a friendly, familiar man with gray hair and tanned, wrinkled skin emerged. He wore faded blue overalls that were covered in grease marks and smudges down the front of them.

"Professor Coleman!" Jack greeted him.

"Well, well, the Joneses! You made it. It's wonderful to see you all again... and you must be Albert? I'm so glad that you could all join me today, and not a minute late." Professor Coleman wiped the sweat from his forehead and signaled to the large clock hanging above the train platforms. It was exactly ten o'clock.

"What are you doing here, Professor?" Emma asked, her voice almost drowned out by the hissing of steam, and the sound of whistles echoing around the station.

Professor Coleman smiled. "So, your parents managed to keep this a surprise? In that case come with me and I'll show you."

Professor Coleman held open the door, inviting his guests into a giant maintenance area. Crews bustled about, shouting over the noise. Machinery whizzed and whirred, metal clanged, and tools and equipment clanked as the workers went about their

6

tasks. The smell of diesel fuel filled the air, as Jack, Emma and Albert watched on in wonder. There were several train engines in the bays, with cranes hanging from the high ceilings overhead.

Despite the hive of activity inside the shed, there was one particular sight that immediately grabbed the group's attention. Ahead of them sat a vintage steam engine, the kind Jack and Emma had seen in their book collection from when they were younger. It was coupled to four matching rail cars, and a caboose.

The engine was red with gold trim and its tender had been painted to match. There was a brass bell and fittings on top of its boiler. Each of the wooden carriages was a cream color with a wide red stripe that ran all the way along the side above and beneath the windows. The caboose at the very end was a deep red with gold stripe.

The train was an impressive sight, even though it looked like it needed some serious maintenance; the paint was dull and faded, and there were lots of dings and dents, no doubt owing to its many years of service.

"Here's my latest project, the Northwest Express!" Professor Coleman announced excitedly. "She's spent the past fifty years in an old railyard shed, and now we've pulled her out and started the process to restore her."

"Whoa, it's amazing." Jack's eyes sparkled as he ran his hand over the dusty nameplate.

"Sure is, they don't build them like this anymore," Professor Coleman replied proudly.

"But it looks a little... uh... old. And like it needs some fresh paint," said Emma.

Professor Coleman chuckled and nodded. "You're right about that, Emma. Restoring a train like this is a big project, she's been here for several weeks while we got the engine back into service again. We've replaced a lot of parts already."

"That sure sounds like a lot of work," said Albert, continuing to admire the engine.

"Yes indeed, this was the best place to get the mechanical things sorted out and once we move her to the railway museum, the restoration of the carriages and all the finishing touches like paintwork and polishing can be completed."

"Well that makes sense, I can't wait to visit the museum and see it all finished!" Emma smiled.

"Of course! You'll all be top of the guestlist I promise, but today I have an even bigger surprise for you."

"Really? Well, what is it?" Jack demanded, he felt like he was about to burst.

"Yes, please tell us!" Emma squeaked.

"Are you going to let us come aboard and take a look?" Albert blurted, his face beaming as he tugged at the straps of his backpack.

"You're getting warmer," Mrs. Jones replied.

"Absolutely!" Professor Coleman cried, "You know, today is a very special day because we're going to relocate the Northwest Express to the railway museum... and I thought you all might like to come along for the ride!"

The children cheered. Jack high-fived Emma and Albert and began to let his mind wander about the adventure that awaited them.

CHAPTER TWO

Professor Coleman led the group into the first passenger car as he shared a little history about the train.

"The Northwest Express is a Class A4 type, originally built in the 1930's to haul express passenger trains. This is the first carriage we're entering now, it's a standard passenger car, as is the one behind it. Then there is an overnight sleeper car, a dining car and finally the caboose, which is quite unique. It was designed for sightseeing so there's great viewing back there! We were very lucky to have been able to put together this combination of carriages—they'll make a great exhibit at the museum."

Everyone nodded.

"Yes, they sure will," agreed Mrs. Jones.

The carriage had a faint odor of coal that blended with the pleasant smell of wood. It made Jack curious. "What's that smell?" he asked.

"That, dear Jack, is the smell of *history*," Mr. Jones answered with a chuckle and everyone laughed.

Theo and Penny Jones were professors of history and archaeology and were always looking to offer their children ways to engage in new experiences and appreciate the past.

"This is certainly an incredible train you've got here." Mr. Jones admired the details of the wood and brass fittings and soft worn leather of the tan-colored seats.

"We were wondering what you had been working on, now I see you've quite possibly outdone yourself once again." Mrs. Jones gushed as she placed her handbag down on one of the front seats in the passenger car.

"Well, thank-you. You know me; once I get going on a project like this, I can get carried away. I traveled on these kinds of trains when I was a boy, probably not much older than you all are now." Professor Coleman smiled at Jack, Emma and Albert. "I loved trains then, and I guess it is an interest that has stuck with me all these years."

"We love riding on trains, too," said Emma excitedly, "but we haven't been on one like this before. I can't wait!"

"Neither can I," said Albert. "Let's go!"

Professor Coleman smiled at the children; he was glad to see them so enthusiastic.

"Okay, we just have one more person to board—the fireman! My friend, Professor Greyson has been working on the project with me. He's in charge of the boiler, and I'll drive the train. And you five are our special passengers, so have a wander and explore the carriages."

"Explore? Now you're talking," said Jack. "This cool train is all ours guys... where should we start?" Jack could barely keep still.

"Well, how about we begin up front?" Professor Coleman suggested. He explained that it would be too cramped for everyone to visit the cab at once, so he would take the children first for a tour, then switch with their parents.

"Perfect! We can enjoy the scenery from back here while we wait," said Mrs. Jones. "You three go ahead and get us underway!"

"Awesome, how do we get there?" Albert asked.

"Well, this is a very special train indeed, in most cases we'd need to stop the train and walk on the platform or ground outside to get from the engine to the passenger compartments, but this tender has a special corridor that lets us go through it!"

"That's so cool, let's go!" cried Jack.

"Right this way then, I need to bend down so I don't bump my head, but I think you three will have a much easier time."

Jack, Emma and Albert followed Professor Coleman as they made their way through a tight corridor and stepped over the gangway where the tender was coupled to the main engine. They were introduced to Professor Greyson who was very friendly and excited to have the children aboard the Northwest Express for her first self-powered voyage in half-a-century.

There wasn't much extra space, but everyone could stand comfortably and watch Professor Coleman and Professor

Greyson set about getting the engine underway.

"I've got the firebox warmed up and she's making steam," Professor Greyson explained. "We're just about ready to go. We have plenty of coal and water, no steam engine can go without both of those... thirsty and hungry these engines are."

Professor Greyson pulled the rope lever to release some steam and the loud, distinctive noise of a train's whistle drew attention from everyone in the maintenance shed, many stopped to gather near the Northwest Express.

Jack, Emma and Albert all waved and smiled excitedly from the driver's cabin as cheers and fist pumps were returned by everyone watching.

Professor Coleman described the various instruments, valves and levers as he and Professor Greyson set about getting them going.

There was hissing and clanking, as well as rattling and groaning from the floor beneath the cabin as the pistons slowly began to pump.

"It's very important to start out slowly." Professor Coleman gently pressed the lever that released steam from the boiler into the cylinders to push the pistons that in turn drove the heavy steel wheels forward. Steam filled the air around them, and thick black exhaust bellowed from the funnel.

The engine groaned as it edged forward, pulling the carriages out of the shed and into the railyard, hissing and clacking as Professor Coleman continued to release more steam.

"We've moving!" Emma shrieked. "Here we go!"

CHAPTER THREE

As the old steam engine chugged out of the railyard and onto the open tracks, Professor Coleman increased the speed and the slow beat of puffs and chuffs sped up into a steady, clickety-clack rhythm.

"Would one of you like to take the controls for a bit?" Professor Coleman shouted to be heard over the engine.

"Would I ever!" yelled Albert with a wide grin. "I love trains, I have a model railway at home—but I never thought I'd ever get a chance to drive a *real* steam engine."

"Well, here's your chance!" Jack encouraged.

Albert stood beside Professor Coleman and took hold of the throttle bar with one hand and the valve gear with the other.

"Most of our journey today is actually going to be uphill. The incline is getting a little steeper now, so why don't you go ahead and release a little more steam; just ease the lever forward a bit more and keep an eye on the steam pressure, here." Professor Coleman pointed to an overhead gauge where the needle was slowly dropping.

"The pressure seems to be going down, is that right?" Albert looked back and forth between the track ahead and the pressure gauge.

"It is indeed. Good spotting, Albert. We're heading uphill now and releasing more steam to maintain our speed—that means we'll need to make some more. Can anyone tell me how we make more steam?"

"I know the answer to that," Jack offered. "We need more coal!"

Professor Coleman nodded. "Exactly! Burning the coal heats the water, which turns it into the steam that makes this whole machine work. Who'd like to help me load some more coal from the tender into the firebox?"

Jack, Emma and Albert took turns to shovel coal from the tender into a small wheelbarrow and then unload it into the firebox.

"Wow, it's so hot in there," Emma remarked as the intense heat from the open firebox filled the cabin.

"It sure is, the fire has to be hot to turn the water into steam in the boiler. See how the pressure gauge is increasing again, now that we've added the coal?"

The trio watched the gauge and nodded in agreement.

Over the sound of the hefty steam engine, Professors Coleman and Greyson gave Jack, Emma and Albert a turn at operating the various valves and levers that controlled the train. It roared along the tracks with a rapid clickety-clack, clickety-clack as the smell of burning coal and grease wafted in the air around them.

"Maybe we should go and check out the rest of the train now?" suggested Jack. "Plus, I'm sure Mom and Dad want a chance to look up here, too?"

"Great idea," replied Emma. "I want to see the caboose! It's such a funny word."

"I want to see all the carriages—is there any food in the dining car?" Albert asked.

Professor Coleman chuckled.

"Unfortunately not... this isn't a regular passenger service. You are most welcome to visit all the carriages, though. There are stepping platforms called gangways between the cars, and you can't really get lost... just don't go any further than the caboose!"

Everyone laughed.

"Do you need any help getting back through the tender?" Professor Greyson asked.

"I think we'll be fine," Jack replied, "we've gotten into—and out of—much tighter spaces before."

"Yeah, this will be like a walk in the park," Albert added with a wink.

"So, what are we waiting for?" Emma giggled.

Professor Coleman tipped his engineer's cap, "Off you go, then. It's a few hours until we reach the railway museum, so take your time and enjoy the ride!"

"Thanks Professor. Let's go!" Jack led the way back to the corridor through the tender.

"Why are you so excited to see the caboose, anyway?" Albert asked Emma as they made their way through the narrow space.

"Hmm... I don't know, it just looked so cute from the platform, like a little mini train car."

The air rushed around them as the three made their way from the tender into the first passenger car. It whistled and whirled as the Northwest Express sped along the tracks.

Mr. and Mrs. Jones looked toward the flurry of wind and activity as the children slid open the squeaky door and entered the car.

"Wow, just *wow*, Mrs. Jones," Albert exclaimed. It's *so* cool up front—Professor Coleman even let me drive the train."

"Now we're going to look at all the other carriages... and the caboose!" Emma said.

"Well, that sounds marvelous," replied Mr. Jones. Try and enjoy the scenery too, we're heading toward those rolling pastures and woodlands off in the distance, and we've even passed a few smaller towns already."

"It really is a beautiful rail route," added Mrs. Jones. "So different from the shorter train trips we've taken to the city."

"Okay, cool. We're off then."

"Don't get lost!" called Mr. Jones.

The children chuckled.

"I guess we'll take our turn up in the engine then, we'll see you all soon." Mr. Jones began walking toward the front of the passenger car and held open the door for Mrs. Jones. "After you, honeypot."

Jack and Emma rolled their eyes and Albert chuckled as they ran off toward the other carriages.

CHAPTER FOUR

"Come on, let's go!" Emma called as she led the way to the back of the passenger car.

The boys didn't need any encouragement as they quickly made their way over the coupling hooks to the next car. The second car was much like the first one, however it smelled a little musty and there were a few rows of seats missing.

"This car's going to need more attention than the first one," joked Albert.

"Professor Coleman said the third carriage is the sleeping car, right?" Emma asked as they opened the door and made their way into the next car, the wind whistling and whirring as they crossed the gangway.

"Yep, that's what it looks like," Jack replied.

"Neat! Bunk beds! How much fun would it be to sleep over on a train?" said Albert as he stepped into one of the private sleeping compartments.

Just as the others followed him in, the train suddenly changed pace and caused the trio to topple over and fall onto the bottom bunk.

"What was *that*?" Emma shrieked as she climbed to her feet and looked out the window.

"Hmm...I think we just rounded a sharp corner," observed Albert. "Lucky that didn't happen when we were crossing between the carriages."

"Yeah, or maybe my dad was driving the train!" Jack giggled as he stood up from the bunk.

Emma and Albert chuckled.

"Come on, let's keep going, we can check out the other compartments, then the dining car, then you know what comes after that!" Emma giggled.

The door that led into the dining car was jammed, but Jack, Emma and Albert tugged, pulled and jiggled it until they managed to slide it open with a loud screech. The dining car was fitted with two rows of tables, two seats on the left and four seats on the right, a serving station in the middle of the carriage and a small kitchen at the end.

Jack went into the kitchen and came out a few moments later wearing a faded apron and a dusty old chef's hat.

"Hey, check this out!" He strutted down the aisle and in his best French accent asked,

"What can I prepare for you? Our specials *du jour* are peanut butter sandwiches and... spaghetti!"

Emma and Albert burst into laughter before following Jack to the kitchen. He returned the hat and apron and they opened a few of the cupboards to look inside.

"There's not much in here—some old knives and forks, but no food or snacks."

"No problem Chef Jack, I'm not hungry yet!" Emma joked. "Can we go and check out the caboose now, *please*?"

"Alrighty, let's go!" Jack replied.

"Hey, have you noticed how much the carriage is angled now?" said Albert. "We must be going up a pretty steep hill."

They stepped with a little more caution along the rattling, angled floor beneath them.

"Yeah, I see that… and feel it." Jack said as he shimmied down the aisle. "I think we've been going up for a while. Look outside, there's mountains nearby now, maybe we're heading up and over them or something."

Suddenly the incline leveled out and the train was horizontal once more. Then, the entire dining car went dark, the clickety-clack continued but the sound of the air whooshing past the train became a hollowed echo.

"What's happening?" asked Emma.

"Um, I think we're going through a tunnel," Albert replied.

"That makes sense," Jack agreed. "I suppose there would normally be lights on in the carriages, but they mustn't be working. I'm sure we'll be through soon."

The darkness was quickly replaced by the bright light of day streaming through the large windows.

"See, like I thought, it was just a tunnel. Looks like we're going *through* the mountains instead of *over* them." Albert grinned. "This train is incredible. Did you know that the Mallard, which is also a Class A4, holds the world record as the fastest steam locomotive?"

"Really? That's so cool," said Jack. His friend sure did know a lot about trains.

Another sharp turn caused all three children to brace themselves against the tables and chairs, so they didn't fall over.

"Geez, what's up with these tracks?" Jack called over the commotion.

"I guess we'd normally be sitting down in one place for most of the trip," Albert offered.

The corner only lasted a few moments before it became easier to stand once more, though the incline returned as the train continued further up the mountain.

"All right, let's check out that caboose before there's another corner or tunnel—or both." Emma chuckled and yanked the door open.

"Good idea!" Jack said as he and Albert followed.

The three children made their way quickly across the gangway and into the caboose.

CHAPTER FIVE

The walls inside the caboose were wooden, and although the shine from the varnish had faded, it still felt like an inviting and important part of rail history. There were bench seats in the middle that faced out toward the large windows. Three tall windows lined the back of the carriage, and there was another viewing seat to take in the passing scenery.

"Hmm...there's really not much in here, is there?" Jack observed.

"True. I guess I didn't really know what I was expecting." Emma walked around the seats, gazing out the windows as she went. "Oh, check this out. If you sit here, you can see where we've been. Look how the track disappears behind us."

"Hey, this is kind of cool." Albert replied as he sat beside Emma. "Did you know that cabooses were originally used on freight trains as shelter for the crew?"

Jack joined them. "You sure know a lot about trains, Albert!"

The kids chuckled and chatted as they chugged past rolling pastures, and Fall colors splashed across the sprawling forest scenery in the distance.

Jack grinned. "These are the best seats on the whole train."

All of a sudden, the caboose lurched hard to the left, and Emma and Albert tumbled toward Jack.

"Corners!" Albert announced as he playfully pushed against Emma and Jack, attempting a 'stacks on' squish as the train turned.

"Oh, I'll get you for this!" Jack joked back as he fought to free himself from beneath his sister and friend.

As quickly as the train had lurched, it straightened out before jolting in the opposite direction.

"Oh, man!" Albert called as Jack made the most of the opportunity to even things up.

"My turn!" laughed Jack as he leaned his weight into Emma which in-turn pushed against Albert.

"Noooo! Why do *I* have to be stuck in the middle?" Emma screeched through a fit of giggles at the commotion.

Just as the train was beginning to level out again, the group heard a loud 'ping' from the armrest Albert had been pushed against.

"Wait, guys. Stop!" Albert cried, but it was too late, the armrest gave way and the three ended up in a heap on the floor.

There was a moment of shock that quickly turned to laughter as they untangled themselves and stood back up.

"I guess you're going to have to apologize to Professor Coleman for that." Jack tried to sound serious.

"Me? But that was your—"

Albert's protest was cut short as he noticed the incline of the track increase again. They all looked toward the front.

"Don't worry, Albert. I'm just kidding around." Jack reassured his friend that he would explain what happened.

"Professor Coleman will totally understand, it will be okay," Emma added with a warm smile. "Why don't we go back up front and see what Mom and Dad are up to?"

"Yeah, before we do any more damage," joked Jack.

The trio began toward the front of the caboose, their steps a little awkward as the train remained on an incline. There was a loud groan which was easily heard even over the constant clickety-clack and whooshing of air that flew past the carriage.

"What was *that*?" asked Albert.

"Hmm... I'm not sure, I think it's a good thing we're—"

CRACK!

SNAP!

Jack, Emma and Albert steadied themselves as they felt the carriage suddenly lose speed.

"Maybe Professor Coleman needs to slow down for something?" Albert suggested.

"Or maybe we're near the museum?" Emma wondered.

"Ah, bad news," Jack called as he raced to the door at the front of the caboose and looked out the window. "The train isn't slowing down, we are!"

"What do you mean?" Albert sounded confused as he hurried to join Jack.

"I think... I think that crack we heard was the coupling. It's broken—see how old and rusty it is?" Jack pointed to the damaged hook on the dining car as it chugged further and further away from them along the track.

"Jack! What can we do?" Emma shrieked with fright. She stood beside her brother, watching the train chugging further away from them up the hill as the caboose continued to slow down.

"Let's not panic," Jack said calmly. "We need to find some way to let the others know what's happened so they can stop the train and come get us."

"Good idea," agreed Albert, "do you have your tablet?"

Jack shook his head "Nope, I left it in my bag at our seats in the passenger car. Anything in your backpack we can use?"

Now Albert looked worried. "No... I've just got some snacks and my lunch."

"I left my bag with yours, Jack!" Emma sighed.

"Well, the good news is that we're slowing down pretty quickly, I guess we can get off and see if there's anything outside that can help us."

"Hate to burst your bubble, but I think the reason we're slowing down so quickly is because we're on a big hill!"

Albert's words flew out of his mouth as he scurried to the rear of the caboose and looked down at the tracks.

"Oh no. Jack, does that mean what I think it means?" Emma sounded worried as she joined Albert at the rear windows.

The caboose came to a brief stop. The air was still, and the children could hear their heavy breathing as the clacking and creaking halted. Then, the caboose began to roll backward.

"Uh-oh. Hold onto something, here we go!" yelled Jack as the caboose set off back down the mountain.

CHAPTER SIX

The caboose began picking up speed as it trundled downward along the tracks.

"How do we stop this thing?" Emma yelled, grabbing onto a handle grip.

"I don't think these cars have brakes, the engine does all of that." Albert answered.

Jack, Emma and Albert stood at the rear windows looking out ahead of them as they continued to roll down the track.

"Well, we're going way too fast now to jump off." Jack watched the ground rush past them.

"Yeah, and we'll probably get hurt really badly if we crash." Emma chewed her lip and fidgeted with her fingers.

"Or we could be derailed, you know... go flying right off the tracks." Albert gulped, "That looks like a sharp corner coming up!" he gasped.

There was some loud rattling and the clickety-clack of the steel wheels on the rails as the caboose approached the corner. The children held their breath as they watched out the windows.

"*Whhhooooa...*" they cried.

The caboose screeched and whooshed around the bend.

"Phew!" Jack huffed once the track straightened out again.

"All right, we made it!" Albert was relieved. "Feels like we're slowing down a bit, the track is flatter here." He pressed his face to the window, his black-rimmed glasses slid down his nose.

"Hey guys, remember that tunnel we went through before? It's just ahead!" Emma squealed, her hands pressing against the glass as she stared into the approaching dark opening.

"That's okay, Em, we'll just roll right through it and out the other side," said Jack.

They each took a deep breath as the caboose wobbled its way into the dark tunnel.

"It's much quieter this time," observed Jack as they rolled through the darkness.

"I guess the sounds of the engine echoing off the walls made it louder before," replied Albert as the soft clickety-clack of the wheels continued along the track.

Emma pointed to the small glow ahead of them. They were almost through, and the light became brighter with each *click* and *clack*.

"It feels like we're slowing down a bit now too, maybe we'll be able to get off once we're out of the tunnel?" Albert thought aloud.

"Great idea!" Jack nodded. "I remember it being pretty steep before we went into the tunnel on the way up, though. So that means we're probably going to speed up again soon. If we slow down enough, maybe we could jump?"

"Yes," said Emma confidently as she peered out the window toward the tunnel entrance. "It would be good to get off before we get too much further away from Mom and Dad."

"Okay, then," nodded Jack, swiping his hand through his hair. "Let's wait by the door and get ready. If there's enough flat ground before it gets steep again, we could all jump together."

Jack, Emma and Albert forced the door open and stood on the gangway.

As they emerged from the tunnel, the children squinted as their eyes adjusted to the daylight. Jack's heart pounded, Emma swallowed the lump in her throat, and Albert wiped the sweat from his palms on his plaid shirt as the wind gushed by them.

Emma's golden hair blew in the wind, and the smell of fresh country air surrounded them.

"We're still going pretty fast." Jack yelled over the noise as the ground rushed by beneath them.

"I want to get off, Jack," Emma moaned.

Albert turned to look in the direction they were heading. "I think we're about to start speeding up again, this is like a roller coaster!"

"It's now or never, I guess." Jack stood at the edge of the gangway, clutching the railing as he dangled one foot over the edge, waiting for the right moment to let go.

CHAPTER SEVEN

"Jack, wait! Don't jump!" Emma yelled, clasping the railing with one hand and grabbing her brother's arm tightly with the other.

The determined look on Jack's face gave way to one of reason. He nodded and stepped back, placing both feet firmly on the gangway outside the caboose.

Before he had a chance to collect himself, he heard Albert's voice.

"Oh *no*, here we go again! It's like we're on a crazy ride at the fun park!" Albert cried as the ground began to slope downward again and the pace of the clickety-clack beneath them picked up once more.

"Let's get back inside and figure out a new plan." Jack yelled over the wind as the caboose picked up more speed. He pushed the door and held it open for Emma and Albert to enter first. Just then a wobble on the track caused Albert to lose his footing.

"Gahh," he yelled as his hands grabbed at the air in search of something to grip. He found Emma's arm and yanked it with urgency, causing her to slip as well.

"Ahhh, help, Jack!" she cried, holding onto Albert so he wouldn't fall while trying not to tumble off herself.

Jack acted quickly. Gripping the railing with one hand, he snatched Emma's other arm to hold her steady.

She wiggled and wobbled but did not let go of Albert, who was doing his best to avoid slipping off the train; he had one leg and half his body hovering dangerously in mid-air! As Emma regained her balance, she managed a firmer grip on Albert's arm, and he was finally able to steady himself and find his footing once more.

"Phew!" breathed Albert as they made their way quickly back inside the caboose.

"Are you both okay?" asked Jack. "I know we want to get off this train, but that really isn't the best way to go about it, you know." He tried some humor as he sensed Albert and Emma were still a little shocked by their dash with danger.

Barely having a moment to catch their breath, the three looked out the window and saw the track ahead of them sloped downward and curved away to the right into a dense forest surrounding the base of the mountains.

"What's that down there?" Albert didn't like what he saw.

"I...I'm not sure..." Jack began as he squinted in the direction of a moving object far in the distance.

"It's another train!" Emma yelped.

Albert could only whisper. "And it's coming right for us!"

Nobody spoke. The sound of the wheels on the track quickened and the wind rushed by the runaway caboose as it roared down the hill toward the oncoming train.

The deep echo of a train whistle in the distance cut the silence.

"They're trying to warn us, but there's nothing we can do!" Albert blurted.

The caboose continued down the hill where heavy forest and thick trees lined either side of the tracks until finally, the ground flattened and slowed them once more.

"Now we can't even see the other train." Jack stared out at the trees whizzing by.

The whistle blasted again. It was louder than before, closer.

"Oh, no!" Emma shrieked and her knuckles turned white as she gripped onto the railing by the window.

"Guys, I'm out of ideas on this one," Jack confessed as his eyes darted around the caboose, searching for anything that might help them avoid a collision.

"Could we try jumping off again?" Albert hardly sounded convinced that leaping from the moving train was a good idea.

Emma shook her head. "No way, we're going too fast."

Jack looked up to the roof of the caboose and pointed to a hatch. "What if we climb up onto the roof?"

Albert looked up. "I don't see how it would help, even if we could get up there, then what?"

"Ahhh, the train is right there!" Emma squealed.

The curve in the track had straightened out and dead ahead of them and bearing down quickly was the train.

"It's a diesel engine, maybe a freight train." Albert said.

"Ah, does knowing the type of train about to crash into us really help?" Jack snapped.

The train's whistle blared frantically, and Emma covered her ears to muffle the near-deafening noise.

The caboose and the diesel freight train hurtled toward each other—clickety-clack, clickety-clack, clickety-clack.

Jack, Emma and Albert looked on helplessly. As the train creaked and the air outside whooshed, the trio huddled together and braced themselves for what was to come. Emma shut her eyes tight, Albert took a deep breath, and Jack gripped onto the others and watched.

With only seconds to spare, the caboose veered to the left, onto another track. It shook hard as the heavy diesel train and its freight cars roared past them, then continued around a bend and out of sight.

"Woo-hoo!" Albert shouted. "The freight train must have signaled somehow to switch us onto a different track!" He jumped up and down and fist-pumped the air.

"Awesome! That was a close call." Jack high-fived his friend. "Where are we heading now though... this track's all overgrown and there's a... oh, man! There's a barricade up ahead, and we're heading right for it!" Jack pointed out the window toward the wooden obstacle ahead of them.

"I guess it's better than crashing into a freight train?" Emma shrugged.

"Well, yeah, that's true..." Jack agreed. "Okay, I think we should sit down and hold onto something, this train is about to go *bump*."

Jack, Emma and Albert sat in their seats and held on tight as the caboose shook and shuddered down the old track.

CHAPTER EIGHT

CRASH! BANG! CLANG!

The caboose became airborne as it smashed through the barricade, sending shattered splinters of wood and glass flying.

There was a final deafening clash as the wheels of the caboose met the rails once more and continued rolling, picking up speed as the track beyond the barricade sloped further downward.

"We're still rolling!" Jack heard the clickety-clack again and felt the rumble of the wheels along the tracks. Jack stood from his seat and headed toward the window. "Watch out for broken glass, okay? Are you hurt?"

"I'm okay. I bumped my arm on the seat when we crashed, and now it's throbbing a bit. But it's not broken or anything." Emma kneeled on the seat and looked out the windows.

Albert sighed as he stood, crunching shards of glass beneath his shoes. "I'm fine, but seriously, where are we going *now*?"

Jack shook his head and shrugged. "Your guess is as good as mine... we're definitely off the beaten track, though. Looks like this one hasn't been used in a long time. It's all overgrown and bumpy... we're in the woods now, too. The good news is that we're not going as fast as before and the track isn't as steep here. But we're still moving way too fast to jump off."

"Even if we did jump, we'd just end up lost in the woods," said Emma. "We're so far away from the others now, how will they ever find us?"

"We'll be all right Em, I promise!" Jack gave his sister a cuddle to help comfort her.

"Hey, look!" said Albert. "There's an old mountain pass up ahead."

Further along was a narrow passageway between the mountains, and the old, bumpy tracks led right into it.

"I wonder what's on the other side?" asked Jack.

"I guess we're about to find out," replied Albert.

"Maybe it's a shortcut to where the Northwest Express is heading? That would be great, right? Actually, I'd be happy to find *any* train station so we can finally get off this runaway caboose!" Emma sighed.

Jack chuckled. "I admire your optimism, Em! I doubt this is a shortcut, but if we do roll into a station, that would be pretty cool. Then someone should be able to help us get in touch with Mom and Dad!"

"That would be great!" Emma smiled.

The caboose trundled along the track, then slowed almost to a complete stop near the top of a small hill. Jack, Emma and Albert looked around and didn't see anything that could help them find their way back to a town or station, so they stayed aboard. The carriage sped up once more as it rolled down the hill and over the other side.

"Hey, is that a building?" Emma pointed out the window.

"I see it!" said Jack. "Good spotting, Em! Looks like there are a few buildings over there!"

"Wow, a town so far away from everything out here in the woods. I wonder where we are?" Albert thought aloud.

"Let's get ready to wave and shout, hopefully we can catch someone's attention while we're rolling through and they can help us off this wild ride." Jack paced back and forth along the windows, searching for anybody that could help them.

The caboose continued to wobble along the uneven tracks, slowing further as the ground beneath them flattened out. As they approached the first buildings, the trio gathered around the windows eager to get a peek at the town and call out for help.

Their hopeful expressions quickly faded as the sight of a crumbling town and a ramshackle station rolled into view.

Albert sighed. "There's nobody here. It looks like the whole town is deserted."

"It's a ghost town," added Jack.

"Hold on to something, boys, there's another barricade ahead," Emma warned.

By now, the caboose was not rolling nearly as quickly and came to a rather uneventful stop, bumping against the barricade with a *bang!*

The sound disturbed a flock of geese, sending them soaring off through the woods, gaggling loudly.

"Well, I guess that's the end of the line!" Albert joked.

"Phew!" Jack laughed. "Who'd have thought that checking out an old train car would turn into such a wild roller coaster ride!" Jack laughed, clutching the back of his neck.

"I know!" Emma agreed. "Let's get off this crazy caboose!"

CHAPTER NINE

The children hopped off the train. Jack began walking toward an old wooden station building nearby, while Emma and Albert looked around the platform.

The station building was rundown and becoming overtaken by weeds and vines. Half of it had collapsed, but Jack noticed a faded old map of the rail line next to the ticket stand, which was still intact.

He brushed away a thick layer of dirt and dust from the glass casing that housed the sign and the map.

He grinned and called to Emma and Albert. "You two aren't going to believe this, but I know where we are."

"Really? Where?" Albert asked.

"We're officially *Nowhere*." Jack giggled.

"What do you mean, Jack? Of course we're *somewhere*," Emma protested.

"Nope, we're definitely Nowhere. Says so right here." Jack pointed to their location on the map.

"A town called Nowhere?" Emma blurted in disbelief, inspecting the map for herself.

"How is that even possible?" Albert scratched his head. "Who would name a town Nowhere?"

"Beats me." Jack shrugged. "Maybe it was someone's idea of a joke, big question is how do we get out of Nowhere and back to somewhere? Somewhere like the rail museum."

Emma and Albert laughed.

"Let's take a look around," said Jack.

"It might be a while before anyone finds us here. Maybe there's a phone or some way to get in touch with Mom and Dad?" Emma suggested.

"Good thinking Em." Jack replied and peered into the ticket window. "That might be a phone in there, let's see if we can get inside."

The door to the ticket office was falling off its hinges so it was easy enough for Jack, Emma and Albert to pry it open. They ventured inside but discovered that the phone didn't work. Jack checked the wire was connected to the plug and jiggled the dial, but it was no use.

The sun was now high overhead in the clear blue sky, casting a warm glow over the mysterious town as the three walked along the main street, stopping at the inn, the saloon and the bank as they went.

Albert cleared his throat and attempted his best cowboy voice. "Feels like we're on the set of an old Wild West movie or something."

Jack and Emma giggled.

They came across the general store and took a look inside. The shelves were bare. Albert offered to share his lunch with Jack and Emma and the three sat on a wobbly bench in the town square and munched on peanut butter sandwiches, cheese and crackers, an apple and some trail mix. Luckily, he also had a large canteen filled with ice-cold water.

"Thanks for sharing your lunch with us, Albert," said Emma when they were done.

"How about we go back to the train station and see what else we can find?"

"Sure thing, Em," replied Albert.

"Yeah, thanks buddy," added Jack, nudging Albert in the arm. "I guess we could always try to walk along the railway tracks until we find another town or station. You know, one that isn't all crumbling and deserted."

"Hmm... maybe." Albert frowned. "But we were in that caboose for a *really* long time and didn't pass anything like that near here."

Jack nodded. "True. All right, let's head to the station, see what we can find and come up with a new plan."

Near the abandoned railway station, the children noticed a side track that led to a large wooden shed. Its red paint was faded and the structure itself needed repair.

There were two large doors at the front, almost as tall as the shed itself, and the tracks disappeared under them.

"Let's have a look in here." Jack pulled on the handles, but the doors refused to budge.

Albert joined in. Together they yanked on the rusty handles, pulling and pushing, jiggling and jerking without success.

Panting and wiping the sweat from their brows, Jack and Albert refused to give in.

"Come on, Albert," Jack called. "One more go. Let's give it everything we've got!"

"Okay, let's do it." Albert replied.

The boys took deep breaths as they positioned themselves and gripped the handles once more, they pushed in a little and then pulled as hard as they could. To their surprise the doors flew open easily and they both found themselves falling backwards and landing on their behinds.

"Whoa! What happened?" Albert asked, squinting and coughing as a cloud of dust swirled around the pair.

"I found another door around the side that was open already. There was a beam of wood locking the two big doors together and I slid it out. I *was* about to call out and tell you…" Emma laughed at the puzzled faces staring back at her.

"Well… thanks, I guess," Jack replied as he stood up and dusted himself off.

"Maybe warn us next time, Em." Albert sounded a little cross.

Emma grinned. "Oh, you'll be fine, and you won't *believe* what's in the shed. Quick, come and see!"

CHAPTER TEN

"No way!" Jack exclaimed. "Check it out!"

Albert whistled. "Incredible. I'll bet Professor Coleman would be amazed to see this!"

Inside the shed was an old steam engine, it's black paint was peeling, the brass trim and fittings were heavily tarnished, and it was covered in layers of dust and cobwebs.

Jack climbed onto the ledge above the wheels beside the boiler and used his hand to clear the name plate. "Chimas 49," he said aloud.

"Wow, a tank engine!" cried Albert. "Check out the big water tanks on both sides of the boiler! I've only ever seen them in pictures, they stopped building these decades ago."

"Really? We have to tell Professor Coleman about it, maybe he can put it in the railway museum, too!" Emma said happily.

Jack jumped down from the ledge, stirring up the dust on the ground as he landed. He rubbed his chin as he looked the engine up and down.

"I have an idea..." Jack began with a mischievous grin. "Why don't we take the Chimas 49 to him?"

"Haha! Jack, that's a great idea!" Emma clapped her hands together. "Do you suppose it still works?"

"Wait a minute," Albert sounded baffled. "You want to try and get this old steam engine working then drive it out of here?"

"Why not?" Jack replied with a shrug. "At worst, it gives us something to do while we wait for someone to find us. At best though... we could drive this all the way to the museum!"

"Oh, we should definitely try! Come on Albert, Professor Coleman taught us a lot, and you know so much about trains already," Emma encouraged.

Albert pondered the idea for a moment. He grinned. "It's unlikely we'll be able to get this going. But, let's see what we can do!"

"That's the spirit, let's get to work!"

The three children wasted no time climbing up into the cab to check things out.

"It's remarkable, all the gauges, levers and valves seem to be in good shape, but the coal bin is empty." Albert recounted Professor

Coleman's lesson about steam engines being hungry and thirsty as they jumped down and tapped on the water tanks. "These are empty too; we need to find water and coal."

"Hey, I saw a water tower outside," said Emma.

"Perfect!" Jack replied. "And hopefully there's some coal stored around here somewhere—it is a train station after all."

"Then we'll have to get the firebox lit and get everything oiled up." Albert continued through the steps needed to bring the Chimas 49 engine back to life.

Jack, Emma and Albert hurried over to the water tower. The steel tank was two-stories high and there was a rusty old ladder leading to the top.

"I hope there's water in it," said Albert.

Jack grinned. "I'll climb up and check it out."

He ran over to the base of the ladder and started climbing, reaching the top in no time. He slowly stepped onto the crumbling wooden walkway that wrapped around the tank.

"This isn't very sturdy," Jack called down.

"Be careful, Jack!" Emma yelled back, shading her eyes from the sun as she looked up.

Jack banged his fist on the water tank. It let out a dull thud.

"Good news!" called Jack. "Sounds like it's full!"

"Great! Now we need to find a way to get the water to the engine. I'll look around for something we can use." Albert headed toward the shed.

"If you're okay to get down by yourself, I'll go and find some coal," said Emma.

"Sure, I'll be fine," Jack replied, waving from the top of the tower.

Emma roamed around in search of coal. She didn't have to look for long. Behind the shed was a coal storage area. There was a wonky old wheelbarrow nearby, which she used to load the first batch. Emma shoveled a heaped pile and wheeled it around to the engine.

"Nice work, Em!" said Jack when he saw his sister's loot. "And I've found an old fire hose that looks long enough to reach the engine from the water tower."

The trio high-fived one another and got stuck into their tasks.

A light breeze blew through the woods as fallen leaves scattered in shades of yellow, red and brown, rustling along the ground. As the children worked, the earthy smell of the forest filled the air and white puffy clouds dotted the blue sky on an otherwise glorious and sunny Fall day.

Jack swung some of the firehose over his shoulder, taking his time as he hauled it up to the top of the water tower. Once he connected it, Albert dragged the other end to the boiler.

"Good news, it reaches!" Albert called out as he removed a kink in the hose.

"Great! I'll turn on the tap!" Jack called back.

Jack struggled to open the rusty valve on the water tower. He gritted his teeth and gripped both hands on the tap until it finally budged.

As the water began to flow through the hose, Albert noticed it was leaking in a few spots.

"Turn it off!" Albert shouted up to Jack who scrambled to shut off the valve before climbing down to inspect the situation.

"Hmmm, I saw some old rags in the shed. I can probably seal it up enough, so we don't lose too much water while we fill the boiler."

"Great, I'll help Emma bring some coal around while I wait," Jack replied.

"Thanks, Jack," Emma smiled. Her cheeks were flushed, and she had black smudges on her chin and forehead. Lugging coal was hard work!

The siblings set off around the shed and used old shovels to fill the wheelbarrow with coal before pushing it slowly along a bumpy dirt path around to the tender where they unloaded it. They were able to bring several loads around by the time Albert told them that he was ready to try the hose again.

Jack headed back up the water tower. This time the spurts of water were reduced to slow drips and Jack climbed back down to continue with the coal, while Albert filled up the boiler and water tank in the tender.

"The boiler and tender are full. Here, let me help with the wheelbarrow, that looks heavy." Albert rolled up his sleeves and set off with the load.

82

The three worked together to fill the firebox and tender with coal for their journey.

CHAPTER ELEVEN

After the tender was loaded, and the boiler and water tank were filled, Albert assembled all the items they needed to get the coal in the firebox burning.

It was a little before three o'clock and the trio enjoyed a refreshing drink of water from Albert's canteen before they climbed into the cab and studied the controls. Soon enough, the heat had caused the temperature and pressure gauges to rise.

"I think we'll be able to start moving now." Albert watched the pressure and remembered what Professor Coleman had said.

"If you say so, Albert!" Emma gave his arm a squeeze.

"You're the train expert, Albert, do you think you can get us underway?"

"Here goes nothing." Albert pressed forward on the lever to let steam out of the boiler and into the pistons.

There was a shudder that shook the whole engine followed by a very load groan.

"What was *that*?" Emma gulped.

"It's been a long time since she's moved anywhere, who knows what will happen. I'm surprised it's moving at all...I'll just take it easy," Albert winked.

The shuddering eased and the groan became a loud *screech*, but wheel-turn by wheel-turn, as the oil greased the rods, the train began to inch forward.

"We're moving Albert! You're doing it!" Jack exclaimed over the noise.

Albert's smile quickly disappeared. "Oh no! We didn't switch the direction to follow the main track up ahead."

"Can you stop the train?" Emma asked.

"May... maybe. I hope so." Albert's mind raced as he took to the levers to prepare to try and stop.

"Wait a second, I'm on it!" Jack yelled as he leapt off the moving train, landing with a thud on the hard, dusty ground.

"Where are you going?" Emma yelled over the rumble.

"To switch the signal!" Jack called back as he ran ahead of the train.

When Jack reached the signal, he pulled on the lever.

It had rusted and was covered with weeds. As the train crept closer, Jack hurried to clear the weeds, then pulled with all his might on the rusty lever.

"I can't stop it in time!" Albert called as the brakes of the engine screeched.

"I'm trying!" shouted Jack, just as the lever finally gave way and the track switched over to join the main line. The Chimas 49 engine puffed safely past the junction.

"Woohoo!" shouted Jack, leaping into the air and fist-pumping it.

"Jack, how are you going to get back on?" Emma shrieked as the train chugged past him.

Jack broke into a sprint, kicking up dust behind him as he ran alongside the engine. Faster and faster he ran as the train chugged along, black soot and steam rising into the air around him.

Jack reached the cab steps and tried to grab hold of the railing. Albert reached out to help pull Jack aboard, their fingers swiped but the train was too quick for Albert to get a good grip of Jack's hand.

"Come on, Jack, you need to run faster," cheered Emma.

Jack bolted until he caught up to Emma and Albert in the cab once more. His legs felt wobbly and his feet ached, but he clenched his jaw and pumped his arms until he was able to grab hold of Albert's wrist. He gripped it tightly, clenched the railing with his other hand, and pulled himself aboard.

Jack panted. "Thanks, Albert! Phew, that was close!"

Albert and Emma patted Jack on the back and smiled.

"Next stop, the railway museum." Albert winked and threw on an engineer's cap he'd found earlier.

The journey was a thrilling adventure, with each of the children taking turns to drive the train. It was much less eventful than their trip down the mountain in the caboose. Albert was able to follow the old rail maps in the cabin to get to where Professor Coleman had shown them, and by staying off the mainline, they were lucky to avoid any other encounters with trains.

As the sun began to set, they approached the rail museum. Mr. and Mrs. Jones, along with Professors Coleman and Greyson came rushing up. All the grown-ups looked relieved, confused and rather stunned to see the children operating a train.

Albert slowed the throttle until they came to a complete stop before they reached the rail museum. Pistons hissed and wheels screeched.

The children jumped down from the driver's compartment. The scenery was beautiful.

There was a lake on one side of the tracks and green hills on the other. Jack's idea to deliver the Chimas 49 engine to Professor Coleman was a success.

"Oh, my! We were so worried about you," said a teary Mrs. Jones.

Mr. Jones smiled. "We've just heard from search and rescue. They've just found the caboose–minus three children! What happened?"

"We've sure got a story to tell you!" cried Emma, cuddling her mother.

"The Chimas 49?" gasped Professor Coleman, reading the nameplate.

"This is an incredible discovery... where did you find it?"

Jack, Emma and Albert looked at one another and grinned. "Oh... Nowhere!"

THE END

JACK JONES

TITLES IN THIS SERIES

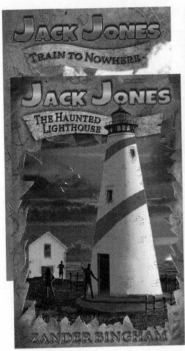

COMING SOON

ABOUT THE AUTHOR

Zander Bingham was born and raised on a boat. It was captured by pirates when he was just 12 years old. He, along with his family and crew, swam to a nearby island where Zander spent his days imagining swashbuckling adventures on the high seas.

Well, not exactly.

But Zander did love boating adventures as a kid. And he always dreamed of exploring deserted islands and being a real-life castaway. He grew up cruising around Australia, the USA and The Bahamas. He eventually captained his very own sailboat, living aboard and exploring the Adriatic Sea with his wife and two young sons.

His thirst for exploration, his witty sense of humor, and his new-found passion for writing stories to read to his boys at bedtime, led to the creation of Jack Jones; the confident, brave and curious boy adventurer who is always searching for his next escapade.